Rana Spring Summer Fall

SHYAM GOHEL

Copyright © 2023 Shyam Gohel

All rights reserved.

CONTENTS

Chapter 1   Pg 1

Chapter 2   Pg 6

Chapter 3   Pg 13

Chapter 4   Pg 18

Chapter 5   Pg 24

Chapter 6   Pg 31

Chapter 7   Pg 36

Chapter 8   Pg 44

1

It's not that it couldn't happen. It's that Rana had done the right thing, and now she'd lost. Not "done the right thing" in an ethical way, but as a human. She'd loved more than she'd tried. Love had been given back to her for every ounce she'd given. Love had been returned to her in leaps and bounds, as if on a perfectly ordinary day when you're walking and looking at the clouds and sky, a wild and graceful creature rushes to you and reaches for your lap, and you never knew such a thing would come running to you. Out of nowhere here was this thing. And this thing is for you. It returns your love even before you had a chance to say your name. If someone told you that this thing was the simple and spontaneous love of a spiritual nature, or if someone told you that this thing that fell into your lap was a unicorn with a mane like a horse and a horn like a bull, it wouldn't have mattered because you thought both were imaginary.

Rana felt like her spiritual mentor had been searching for her since before she was born. It was a love that waits for you. A love easily misunderstood as being attractive, just as the ancient Indian rhinoceros has been misunderstood as the allegory of the unicorn. This love Rana felt had a weight like a rhinoceros. A spiritual type of love weighs on you. It waits for you. It waits for you as the earth waits for you. The way that the mass of a rhinoceros creates gravity.

A rhinoceros

is the best picture

we have

of what gravity is.

The love of Rana's life was not a person among persons, but a gravity. She hadn't intended to love that much. But she kept falling through. She recognized her spiritual mentor to be a true one, a real one. The kind that never takes. The kind that only returns to you what is yours. Something she hadn't believed existed on earth. It was all rhinoceros. It was a spiritual love for a being you thought was imaginary.

Rana had spent time with her spiritual mentor. Then more and more time. Rana saw the mentor day by day, hour after hour, went to the doctor with the mentor, went to physical therapy with the mentor, had gone on travels near and far, by road and over seas, with the mentor, ate with, cooked for the mentor. She had massaged this beautiful creature's feet and legs, sat at the mentor's feet, the way you read about, like they did in ancient times or something. Rana looked at the mentor the way you imagine birds spread their wings, stretched out their necks and gazed at St Francis. Rana travelled to holy places with her mentor, and she found that the holy thing in the holy place was the tunic of the mentor.

Rana worked morning to evening for the mentor. She cried when her insecurities and her bravado hurt the mentor the way we all get hurt. She laughed with her spiritual mentor ten times every day, like for real ten times a day at least. Rana could make her mentor laugh, too, like really laugh, at least once a day, usually at something really silly, a kid, a quip, like it wasn't funny funny but it was hard not to laugh. The way Rana saw the world she saw the comedy deep within things. In all things, the heart is a contradiction. We try to protect our hearts but it's not really ours. Nothing is ours in the way we think it's ours. Rana saw her mentor sometimes delight like a child with nothing in hand, nothing to gain or lose. Sometimes the spiritual mentor had a royal quality, like a dignified nature, in the way that being adorned with no material things has a majesty to it. The way an elk has majesty. Or a mountain, or a desert, or a frog. Things are ours to gain when we don't have them. To have a thing is to grow a thing. When you love something, you make it gain weight.

And all this love, like a jar full of bliss, had been given to Rana in return for her hunch that everything everyone promised her from the beginning probably wouldn't work out, and that

that wasn't anyone's fault. That was just the way things were when your belief is that things fall to the earth because things belong on the earth, and you don't know about gravity. You don't know why a rhinoceros bears all her weight close to the earth. When you know that things don't belong anywhere, there is no home and there is no foreign land, you feel that weight. You feel alone. And you have a connection to fallen things.

Anyway, those are all feelings.

2

Rana's spiritual mentor left this world. It was the thing Rana knew would happen one day, but never thought it would actually happen. There was a simple ceremony. Like all material things, the material stuff was burned to ash. When you're grieving, it sometimes feels like you're so thrown inside yourself that you don't walk on the earth anymore. You don't feel the ground of the earth. You wish that each step you take could be a step backwards.

But when fire turns the material stuff to ash, you feel something else, too. You feel like all the immaterial stuff also goes back to their sources. Like, the laughter is material, but the sentiment behind the laughs, the liberated sense, the unburdening feeling of the mood of laughter, Rana felt, is free to return to its origins. She and so many others who had the mentor's blessing felt an expansiveness of heart, too. For the children of God come and exist for the children of the earth. Kind of like how we're the source of mathematics and all the beauty of the stars and skies and yet they exist without us, too.

Rana wondered what her spiritual mentor would have her do with her life.

It took years for her to realize that it was

what was

always wanted.

Her spiritual mentor would want her to do the simple thing she was asked to do from the beginning.

Which was

A kind of sincerity and yearning in her prayer, and the repeating of the name of God she received.

To hold onto it and make it grow.

To make it grow and wait for it to grow, like how you exact a promise.

Rana was walking along the St Francis river when she was thinking of all this. What had been asked of her to do with her life was this promise. A promise that's not a deficit but an undertaking.

On that day, when she was walking on the St Francis river thinking all this, Rana sent me a postcard. She doodled a river and circle, and wrote –

> Winter
>
> Animals slow their hearts in winter
> Do the same
> Find shelter
> Don't move
> Breathe slow and linger
> Then start with the dust
> And cinder

I wrote back to her –

> You know, I've been thinking about things. Reality isn't so much about truths. It's about desires.
>
> For example, if you say that the stone wants to be on the ground by its very nature, and not by the law of nature, you make something that's compelled by law something that's desired by the thing.
>
> You could then say that the thing desires the law.
>
> If the thing desires the law, then you could have the thing that is not the law. That is, things are not where they are by law because they are where they are by grace. But if law has room for grace, then it's not grace. Therefore, grace is the thing that the law desires.
>
> Anyway.
>
> Question, Rana, if you overhear something
>
> Is it speaking to you
>
> Is it speaking to you
>
> Is it speaking to you

Rana didn't write back.

Rana thought of what she liked in this world, walking on the water, on the St Francis. What she did for fun. What she wanted the outside of her life to look like. What it could look like. Rana liked to be carried. It would be hard to look inside herself and find something that pushed her towards her fate. Rana liked to be taken with. Like when you see a spider in her web on your wing mirror, and you take her with you. If you told a spider you loved, that she feels like home for you, she wouldn't understand the romance of it.

Rana was there, on the waters, of the St Francis, walking, with the ashes, of her spiritual mentor. She gets on a boat. The ashes go in the water. It really was like a clean wash. A free ending. I don't know if you've ever had this feeling. You felt emptied, you were emptying, and it was joyful and crushing at the same time. Nothing dramatic. I wouldn't call it an event. It was like a tear falling in the river, and the tear being in the river without being the river. It was like a healing painful feeling.

Rana had had the ashes in a small wooden box.

The ashes and the box went in the river. The box came out of the river.

Some days later, Rana found a thistle of ashes dried up in the box. Like a pinch or two.

Rana went through her things to find this locket necklace she had. The ashes she put as much as she could inside there. Whatever ashes stuck to her hands, Rana brushed her hands on her forehead, through her hair, behind her ears, a touch inside her nose, a touch between her eyebrows, and on her tongue. It was one of those moments you don't know if you're doing the thing that's inspired and grieving, or if you're acting out something, an artistic act, something dramatic and meaningful, something a creature would do naturally, like a cat covering herself under ashes. Rana smudged a bit of the ashes between her toes and under her feet. Rana thought she wouldn't touch the earth except through the ashes.

Rana rested her hands on her face. Her fingers on her eyelids. For a long time. Like seven minutes. Maybe the whole thing took nine minutes.

You know when you think you'll feel renewed

and lighter, but you just have more energy to put into the same things you were thinking and doing.

3

Rana came away from the waters. Not feeling so alone.

She opened and closed the locket a thousand times for the next hundred days.

She would return the ashes back to the earth. When she tried to immerse all the ashes in the river, the river took as much as she wanted. The rest she left as a secret ingredient for Rana to prepare a new way of taking interest in things.

So many times Rana had seen from her window the pottery studio across the street. So many kids coming in and out. Rana couldn't see their faces from her window. She saw the tops of their heads. She liked how kids usually had no part in their hair, it was all just there. The kids were mostly hair, crumbs, and energy like you couldn't believe. Sometimes they seemed like purely spiritual creatures, exempt from all laws of all continents. Rana saw the kids sometimes going from having a complete meltdown, literally creating around them a radius of mass destruction and extinction, to having the brightest smiles and wide eyes you'd ever seen, as if they were hearing deep in their souls reggae music for the first time. Like you never knew life could be so good.

Rana walked to the pottery studio. She ducked her head as she entered the door. It wasn't a bow. Even though she thought it was. It was more like she was making herself small.

Rana told the pottery studio she had no money, she had ashes. To return to the earth. Etc. Etc. She thought she could start with a clay. Maybe make a small pot or something. She wanted to feel her hands and legs on something. Rana was nervous saying all this for the first time out loud. She wanted a new beginning, she said. After all, the pottery wheel was the invention of the wheel, she said, wasn't it. A symbol of continuing on and also of returning. Invented by the same earliest of civilizations between the two great rivers that also invented study of the eternal motion of the stars in the sky. Rana couldn't remember if the spinning wheel was invented in the same region or if it was in neighboring India. Anyway, she said. These aren't feelings.

The studio gave Rana some free time for all the steps. She added a bit of her ashes to the clay and started wedging. She took time getting seated behind the wheel, anchoring her elbows, throwing, centering, squeezing the clay, pushing down and in, which is all part of centering. It all happened so fast. The wheel was so fast. She honestly thought she'd be using her feet to spin the wheel, maybe with a pedal. She thought she would be on her own time, moving at her own pace.

The pottery wheel, for Rana, was too much. It made a sharp, high sound. She opened the clay. She tried to raise the walls. But it wasn't a good idea, Rana thought. She didn't like being hunched over, facing down. Maybe the children were able to stand up and look straight ahead when they worked on the clay. Rana didn't clean up the mud. She liked the idea of weakened walls. If she cleaned up, what if the excess clay had the excess ashes in it? Kids didn't have excess things like that. They kept and dropped things as if that's how you were supposed to handle them. Kids dropped things before they handled them.

Rana stared at her walls and thought that if you could feel the celestial spheres spin, or if you could feel the earth spin, and if you could hold it in your hands, you wouldn't feel like shaping it. You would feel like bracing for it. Let it press against you, she said. Like when your dog leans into your legs for affection. It's a gravity.

With a wire, Rana cut the clay off the wheel.

Rana didn't want to become too attached to the clay. She would let it dry in the sun for four or five weeks, in the meantime of which, the kids had come and gone to their pottery classes. They created and destroyed whole worlds every other day. It's like when a child swallows dirt, and you ask her to open her mouth, and you see a whole world in there. You didn't know someone so small could have inside her mouth something so infinite, like how Pinocchio felt in the belly of the whale, he had a whole world in there. The belly of a whale isn't so much a place but a time, to rest. Children eat and shape earth to rest. Isn't it so, Rana thought. She laughed. She thought it was funny. Children eat dirt to rest. She really thought it was really funny. And laughed.

Rana's pottery vessel sat outside drying in the sun. It didn't hold together for long. She thought she saw footprints of birds on the trim. Who knew birds weighed so much.

4

Rana could draw. She liked when lines made things. It was borderline miraculous how lines made things. You could draw things you couldn't explain. You could divide up the earth with lines if you wanted to. God seems to have set the world in motion with simple lines and shapes. Isaac Newton said that ten moons are revolved about the earth. The ten moons, he said, were infinities you could govern with an understanding of lines. But, Newton said, graces and laws are not infinities, they are infinite. It's not a question of their being but a question of their nature. Their nature is infinite. The Supreme God and gravity, he said, are infinite. There was more to understand about them than all the lines and passages in the world. The infinite, like a promise, has a beginning but no end. Rana wanted to think that even a rhinoceros, like a promise, is infinite. But she wasn't sure.

It would be nice to try painting, Rana thought. Rana had had a friend who once painted for her the face of Buddha on a pizza box cover. That was probably seven years ago. The friend had also painted her a leopard out of small dots that glowed in the dark at night somehow. She'd get scared at night of the cat. Rana couldn't remember which aspect of the Divine Mother rode on a leopard. Lion, yes, tiger, yes. The painted leopard wore roses with green eyes and a pretty mouth, companion of Dionysus, god of the arts and rage. That was not how Rana was feeling. It wasn't rage. Neither did she feel the searching and the serenity of Buddha. Rana thought she'd paint how she was feeling. Not paint a feeling, but how. She'd paint the sunset she saw every day, around a little after five in the evening, or sometimes after six. Rana had had in her twenties a wonderful older friend who was a librarian in the kids' section of the nearby library. The friend moved to the west to live with her family when she ran out of money. Rana always liked the library and made her way there. She didn't know if there were adult painting classes. She went to the kids' section.

The kids' painting class was before lunch time. Rana sat on the floor with her paints and papers on the floor. The kids were on the floor, their paints and papers on their tables. Rana quietly joined them. She didn't say anything. She didn't ask permission by asking for permission. She asked permission by ducking her head into her chest and couching down and making herself small. The kids saw her. Rana smiled. She smiled and laughed through her nose, as if to tell the kids, hey don't get me in trouble. Sometimes Rana asked the kids what they thought of the colors she used. She started with color pencils. Started from the bottom. A little less than half the page became a blue mist, like a streaky blue mist. Into a little coral or pinkish orangish space with empty spaces for clouds. Then a few swipes of faint reddish clayish earthish color. Then a bright yellow. So, from the bottom, blue, coral, pink, red, yellow. Rana kept being told by the children to paint a robot dinosaur, a jellybean fish, a platoon, a gafoon, a baboon, five baboons, twenty baboons, a hamster earring, and a palace of frozen juniper lions singing a la-di-da-di-di la-di-da-di-lu. One child told Rana to paint the whole sky as the whole earth.

Rana heard from the children she could paint circles and circles and circles. Or spots on spots on dots, lots of them, as if the sky was a huge doormat, and we were only going in or out of this and that world. Rana could draw a bowl the size of a mouth that did not breath air but only buttons. Paint a floating image of a shade of a woman unwinding along a winding path, the woman becomes a bird of gold and dances on the sleeves of a dolphin's frock, and all this underneath a huge flood. Rana thought of drawing Italy with reds, black, golden light, spilled coffee, and smiles.

Rana finished her pencil sketch with a lighter yellow above the bright yellow. Then, continuing from the bottom up, she drew the same pattern in reverse order. A teeny red, very little pink and coral, and blue. She liked the lightness of it all. There really wasn't a sun in her sunset drawing.

Sketch done.

Now paint.

With the weight of the paint on her brush, Rana felt heavier. No soft sunset. Nothing pretty or darling. She would paint a matador. She wanted blood. She started with a bull. Her bull looked like an obedient rhinoceros with no armor, eyes closed, a rectangle, or series of lovely blotchy earth browns and dirty yellows, bowing at the feet of the matador. The matador was the bull's fate. "Bull at the feet of fate," the painting was called. The animal looked like it was conspiring with its destiny. Rana's painting of the bull was of that loving resignation. That's how she felt. She painted that.

Rana wasn't exactly sure what a matador was. She mixed the tiniest pinch of her ashes into the paint, and evenly colored a horse for the matador to ride high high up. The matador was not a matador but a rejoneador. The swan neck of her horse looked as elegant as a seahorse. The rejoneador's horse stood tall, head up high high, taking pride in the bull's submission, this act of the bull's absolute freedom. The bull was no longer a wretched animal to be conquered. With its feet in the ground, head to the ground, the bull was an image of gravity. The bull was a creature of the Lord, heavy, like an infinite rhinoceros. The rejoneador herself was a terrible red, bloody, blushing, heated, scared fellow, almost having nothing to do with the conversation of the animals. The rejoneador uses her weapon simply to balance herself on the horse who has come to a sudden halt at the appearance of a sacred creature asking for her end to come with certainty.

Rana's painting was in no particular style of art. It was a grand sweep of blotches and strokes. Vivid reds, yellows, browns, and black intrusions on a very plain large page. When you saw the painting, you got the feeling there was something happening that only animals understood. These are creatures whose lives are guided by a search for wild freedom. Their submission is their final act of resistance. The painting is of two creatures sharing in the kindness of fate. Rana changed the title to "Kindness of fate."

5

Rana took a class at the library on script writing. Rana had been able to mix some ashes into her clay and paint. Now her clays and paints would be her imagination. St Augustine said that the image is not a thing but the promise of a thing. An image of a thing, he said, is the promise of the thing's blessedness, like how we are made in the image of blessedness. Ethical life, he said, was to be, know, and love this empty promise at the expense of everything else in this world. It may seem unreasonable to hold on to the image of a thing instead of the thing. But that's how Rana was feeling. She felt that the ashes she carried were the promise of her fate. And, Rana felt that she was the image of the ashes.

Rana wrote a short comedy in the morning, and a short drama in the evening.

Comedy

(2 characters, Delilah and Soniya, Delilah comes home from work)

Delilah: Oh my. (Laughter)

Soniya: I'm so sorry. (Laughter)

Delilah: It's not your fault, my love. (Laughter)

Soniya: I can see you're shaken. Shall I stir a fresh lemonade? (Laughter)

Delilah: You. (Laughter) Thank you. (Laughter)

Soniya: Why thank you. (Laughter)

Delilah: Just because. (Laughter)

Soniya: Kids having a hard time accepting love and forgiveness again, at work? My love? (Laughter)

Delilah: The child will at one time or another in one form or another argue for you not to love them. (Laughter)

Soniya: Is that different from old fashioned acting out? Or rebelling? The way we used to when we were kids? We were kids, too, right, at one time? (Laughter)

Delilah: Art is one of the only places we get to practice breaking completely apart, you know? (Laughter) We don't need to fall apart in the right way, you know? Art is the place to fall apart absolutely. (Gasps) So you can't be put back together again (laughter) in the same way.

Soniya: The way every science lab is an improv troupe? (Laughter)

Delilah: My children whom I see every day see themselves as the trauma that happened to them. The funny thing is (laughter) that the trauma is real, it's their sense of self that's unreal. (Laughter) There's no personal sense of self before the self gets injured. When you know that the self has deficits, you start to live as who you are.

Soniya: So they yell at you because they think you're removing their trauma? You're not! (Laughter)

Delilah: Maybe. (Laughter) It's hard to explain that we don't try to love the trauma. We try to love the deficit. It's a deficit that's also an excess. The deficit is an excess because it wasn't there there, you know? The deficit is the one thing in them that they can never lose. It's who we all are. (Chuckle) The deficit is not an experience among experiences. It's more formal. It's how the self is shaped. How many more ways can I say the same thing?! (Laughter) It's hard, I know. (Calm laughter)

Soniya: So when we give up on the image of a completely formed self, then there's the possibility of growth and pain? (Gasps) But these are just ideas. What are the feelings? (Applause)

Delilah: Loss. The self is a series in loss. It's also why when someone loves you, you say, "All this for me?" and you grieve the world you've created, the world in which you've made yourself small. (Applause)

Soniya: Don't you believe we're created in the image of God, my love? (Laughter)

Delilah: I don't know about God, or if we're created by God. But, yes, we are the image of God. (Gasps)

Soniya: So then what God lacks is our love, my love? (Laughter) God lacks faith in God? (Laughter)

Delilah (laughing): Only if God isn't also the image of God. (Applause)

Soniya: I don't get it. (Laughter)

Delilah: I believe in the image of God. When we're there for each other without having to invent some reason. When we're just there. That's the image of God. It's the image of God that is our faith in God.

Drama

(2 characters, Delilah and Soniya)

Delilah: I can't take it anymore!

Soniya: Problems! Problems! Nonstop problems!

Delilah: I love you, my darling.

Soniya: There's something I need to tell you.

Delilah: There's something I need to tell you, my darling.

Soniya: If there were no suffering, would music even be interesting?

Delilah: You come to me? You tell me that?

Soniya: Let's just enjoy this moment.

Delilah: Why won't you love me, my darling?

Soniya: Love is the one thing I cannot give, my darling. You always find that you've already given away your love when you try to love. It's already been taken from you. The other already has it before you've given it.

Delilah: I throw myself at you, my darling.

Soniya: Shall I be loved and not feel loved?

Delilah: I feel loved. Therefore, you love me.

Soniya: Therefore, you are loved. But love is not what you want. You want me.

Delilah: Is that so wrong?

Soniya: I embrace you, my darling.

Delilah: My love, don't say that.

Soniya: I much prefer the uncertainties of love. To be one step away from complete dissolution.

Delilah: That's not profound. That's just the thrill of the chase.

Soniya: No! Never say that, Delilah. You're leaving me now?

Delilah: You wouldn't even have had to ask. I would have scolded you if you thought of being miserable without me.

Soniya: That's not promising for you.

Delilah: That's not promising. That's love. (Crying)

6

Even when the gods finish their works of imagination, they want to shake the earth and move their feet. A poem is a traveler. Our voices and feet are more or less up to the same things.

Rana rubbed a smidge of ashes between her toes, laced up her shoes, drew wings on the sides of them, she hit the ground, slapped the ground, grunted, laughed, and went to the park to ask to be a part of the Hermes running program, where you could run with someone who was blind, and the two of you would hold onto a small rope-like thing, and you feel it out in stride.

On the run, Rana listened all about people's lives. One person was an elementary school music teacher. One person ran away from home about ten years ago. She didn't know how to tell her family that she loved them, and that they needed to let her go for a while. Rana met one woman who read the full Proust every year. Another younger person said he was learning how to cook and be a chef maybe one day. One time Rana thought the person she was jogging with was blind, and that person thought that Rana was blind. They didn't realize it for a long time until Rana said, "I'm jealous of your outfit, hon. I love to dress like a rhinoceros. You see my updo? My mystic horn? But your pink top and red bottom with black cap. You look like a brilliant matador. I'll bring you a yellow handkerchief next time." And the woman said, "I love how your updo brings out the full shape of your ears. You ever wish your ears were above your head?"

Sometimes, the conversation was about Rana's children, if she had any children, and why she didn't. Rana said she never imagined herself at this age without kids. She never imagined herself at this age with kids either. Rana just never thought of her future much. It was not a skill she had. She sort of just waited to step into her future. Her future would ask her to follow, and she would try to wade through it if she didn't fall through. She didn't know that she would be making her future all along the way. Maybe twenty years ago Rana decided she would dedicate herself to serving her spiritual mentor until the final day. When the day came, the next four or five years went by without any kind of feeling. She wished for heartache and rage. But there was nothing but time. Rana waited a few more years waiting for the bottom of earth to have her and keep her and know her and love her. She'd been searching for some weight to pull on her. Rana didn't know that you couldn't just let gravity take you. Gravity would only take you if you wanted to go somewhere, and gravity would get you there.

Rana had forever thought of adopting some teenagers. "You pour love into them in torrents," Rana said, "and you're not invincible, so when you're hurt or worried, you tell them how you feel. The rest is up to the fates." "I've learned,"

Rana said, "the best you can do is show up, take the good with the bad, and know that only your God and your spiritual mentor are behind you. I'm not saying that all the rest of the world is against you. But it can feel like that pretty often."

People would ask, "That's why you don't have kids?" Rana laughed and would say, "I get all wound up. I make circle after circle around my own self. I guess I don't have kids because I just never had the chance. And I didn't have the chance because I didn't know that if I didn't make it happen, it wouldn't happen. Not that I was dying to make it happen. I'm not dying for much of anything right now. I'm running now. I have a future before me for the first time in my life, and it's scary. Because it's all up to me. My God and my mentor are the kind of people who only do good for me, but they're the kind of people who want me to make my own fate even if it goes against the fate planned for me — that's the only way to learn who I am and what I can do. I have the skills to submit, surrender, mourn and be insulted because of my faith. Those skills only come alive if you charge towards your matador. You know?"

One time someone told Rana, "Don't believe

what people say, my dear. Teens are easy to love." Another person told her, "You've got the right idea, kiddo. Loving yourself is overrated. Go after something."

7

Rana asked around if she could pick up some work babysitting. She'd never really done it before. It was terrifying.

You know when a child looks at you,

and keeps looking at you,

until you realize,

that she realizes,

that you're nothing

but panic and bones.

Rana saw the child's eyes looking at her.

Rana couldn't answer the child's simplest questions. Why was Rana's name Rana?

Rana's name said nothing, was nothing, meant nothing.

Rana felt embarrassed to point around the room at things and name them for the child to learn what those things were, as if pointing to something orange and saying orange said anything about what colors are to us. Things are not what they are because that's what they are when we say so. Things are what they are because they are seen as beautiful. And beauty is not an element of what is true or what is good. What is true is true because it is good; and what is good is good because it is beautiful. And how to see beauty is the nature of play. Like the playtime of a child who for no reason, and no good reason, laughs and cries and plays. When a child looks and points, as she often does, Rana liked to believe, she was pointing to where she wanted you to take her.

Rana taught herself to lean in and touch her forehead to the forehead of the child. She would look into the child's eyes as if a whole world was forming, as if moons were forming their orbits around the two of them. When you pay attention to the child, you allow her to be a gravity, and that lets her walk the earth knowing that the earth will go to her when she falls.

Rana spoke to the child, asked the child question after question, answered the child's own questions. None of this for the purpose of learning.

Words were meant as a measure of distance. The sound of words told the child how close Rana felt to the child.

Worlds form by pushing things away. Give a child some space, and she can conduct her world, the way a piano player conducts her own time. And time is all that determines how we feel.

In this way, all the sights and sounds Rana and the child shared were different ways to engage the feelings of the child, the touch of things, the sensation, and all the emotions of it, how you let it affect you. Touch is the language of the child. Touch reveals that our bodies and bones are not bodies and bones. They are emotions.

Part of Rana's job as a babysitter, she felt, was the teaching of aloneness. How to be alone. And why. Not all the time. But sometimes you're alone.

When you're alone, it's the perfect time to practice giving yourself away, Rana thought. If you don't practice this, you'll strive to have a strong sense of self, be self-fulfilled, and feel terribly alone. And you won't know why. But if you give yourself away, you create a kind of self for yourself that is for the purpose of giving. That kind of aloneness doesn't weigh on you. That kind of aloneness becomes time for you to remember all the things you have to offer, and what it is you want to make of yourself, where you would like to go. Being alone becomes your time.

The one thing you can't have is yourself. Rana always thought of what Borges had said: something like, you can only give away what is already the other's. You sometimes feel like you intrude into a child's world, or you sometimes feel like you don't want to intrude into her world. But usually, the child has already given a meaning to your intrusion before you can introduce yourself as who you wanted to introduce yourself as. That's how children welcome you. And that's why their welcomes can be menacing, too. You can never intrude because you're already late to the welcome. The game is happening before the start. If you try to fake an understanding of the game, children will usually see that you don't see what isn't there to be seen, but is there to be felt and tackled.

These are all just thoughts.

"Mostly croissants and cheese" is how Rana described her babysitting strategy. She liked to get the kids on the move. Babysitting became going for a stroll. They played the game, "What's that? Tree, animal, bird, or robot?" Another game was "Are they playing or fighting?" Another game was, "Where shall we sit and eat?"

Rana was sometimes asked to tutor the older kids while babysitting the younger ones.

Rana called tutoring doing homework.

Babysitting she called sitting.

A rhinoceros will pretty much spend her whole

life doing homework and sitting, teaching her kids to be alone and independent. Alone really is a big word for being free. Alone is a big word for love. Love plus teaching is the right kind of alone. A rhinoceros teaches through love to be alone. It's the kind of alone you feel when you put yourself between a child and something that harms the child. It's that kind of alone when you say, I am all that exists for you, I am your path to be free, and I am your path to be frustrated, and if I do my job right, you will feel that all that exists is you.

And yet. Even with all this teaching. All this teaching. If a mother rhinoceros loses her child, she will lie in mourning in a bend, blinking her eyes and moving her ears in disbelief, her body will be foreign to her, she won't be able to stand, she won't look forward to anything, let alone things going back to normal, she cries and cries, she won't be able to hide her grief, and yet all her grief is inside her, she dreams of her lost child, thinks of the child's touch, smell, remembers her squeaks, sounds, and songs, she sees the places her child walked, where her child sat, what her child ate, how she ate, how she walked, how she slept, how her child breathed, and how she tried to make her child feel calm and loved, excited and loved. The rhinoceros sometimes wonders if her child knew she was dying, if she felt alone in a scared way, and if the child was able to think of God before her last moments.

Rana made sure the homework got done. She asked the kids questions and questions to guide them towards their own way of thinking things through. Being asked questions and questions is the kind of play that can really get to you, make you beyond frustrated and mad. That's why Rana got the homework done first. Then came the learning. Homework got the answers. Thinking got the kids to answer. When you get completely frustrated in your thinking and just wish someone would tell you the answer, that's when Rana got silent. A teacher lets a person be alone. The teacher stops and stands nearby. The teacher does nothing at that time but stand in between the student and harm's way, like every rhinoceros does naturally.

Rana wanted her kids to take an interest in themselves. She wanted them to hear what they themselves say, and like how they say what they say. She liked her kids to be bold in their thinking up until the point when they realize that kindness is often a higher kind of thinking. Ethics is always the first form of thinking. Ethics is a wonderful kind of aloneness.

Ethics is to be unafraid to not be like everyone. To be alone in thought. To give others a moment to think.

Rana wasn't sure she could be a teacher. Teachers stand tall. Even when they bow, they stand tall. They walk in a room, and you remember the first time you saw them, or the first time you remember seeing them. You remember how they listen to you. They look at you when they listen to you. It's as if their feeling of care for you and time itself become the same thing. Time is no longer passing moments but care itself. The teacher hints to you something like there will be rough winds and seas ahead. The waters may get so turbulent you think your boat will drown, the teacher says. When you hear of this allegory of your own emotional life, you feel that the teacher is there already on the other side of it. You don't always feel the teacher is with you. You feel the teacher is waiting for you.

8

It's been nine years since Rana was last on the waters of the St Francis. Rana decides to stay there for some time. She likes the water. She likes the weight of the water. If you're afraid, you can feel lost at sea even if you're only a few feet from the ground. Rana thought that you get afraid if you don't take a moment to feel the water. The water keeps moving you, and if you feel pushed around, you panic.

Rana practiced wading in the water.

Like a rhinoceros.

She gained weight.

She went in the river.

She didn't swim to get anywhere. There was no race. No clock. No time. She often bobbed in and out. You know when you see animals on the water half in half out. Half under half above. That was Rana. She considered it swimming even if your feet were touching the bottom. Walking in the water was swimming. Jumping in the water and letting the river catch you was swimming. It was all swimming. If there was water, and you were there, and you were in it, it was swimming. Somehow you don't feel separateness in the water. You don't think that body, mind, and soul are different things. They are different feelings you have. And in the water, all feelings are true. Water brings them together. You know you're not at home in the water. You're always traveling in the water. It's all swimming to Rana.

After a while, Rana learned a little boating, and got a small canoelike thing. She sent me some business cards she wrote out with color pencils and cut with scissors, "Rana Float Swim Wade." It made me laugh. Rana float swim wade. It wasn't a business. It was a string of words you could hand someone to remind her you're around to go out with her on the water. Rana would take you out on the small canoelike boat. You could paddle and learn a little boating from her. You didn't have to paddle. You didn't have to learn. You could just float and look at the sky. You could go for a swim. You could just be in the water half under half above.

Rana would go out on very calm days when there was no weather. The St Francis river was not far across. You could go across and come back by the end of the day. No real rough rocks anywhere. If you traveled west, that's probably the way you came. Most people who took Rana up on her offer went east. It looked like the river would narrow as you went east. But pretty quickly you saw that what you thought was a part of the land was an island. The river opened up. Wide open. All directions seemed the same in the open. In fact, open is also a direction. When someone asked Rana what to do now that we're in the open, she said they could sit in the middle of the water. Do nothing. Be there. You could get out and swim or bob. We could talk about something.

We could read. You could read. Or write. Pray. Sing. Come back anytime. With a friend, or a daughter, or alone.

There was a sacred aspect to being near water. Something about being in nature, with the animals, being on land, being in the water, looking at the sky. It made you feel small and alone but surrounded by love and contemplation. You were reminded that you were too small and alone for nature to want to drown you if you didn't want to be drowned. In that mysterious way, nature cared for the least of things.

Rana liked to think of her time on the St Francis as a feeling of retreat. It wasn't a retreat of departure. It wasn't anything as momentous as a turning point.

Rana's retreat was the remembrance of a forgotten beauty. The soft beauty of things that wait for you and ask you to rest. Retreat is a time for writing letters, for thinking of mentors, and being awake.

I used to think that beauty was the radiance of a thing. I thought that beauty was the warmth and brilliance of things that made you see a thing as there for you.

Rana said that beauty was the awakening of things. She said that the awakening of things was everything a mentor could do for you. A mentor would promise to protect you. It was for you to look around, and wander alone for a while sometimes.

If she had some time, and the person joining her on Rana Float Swim Wade was okay with it, Rana would take a quick splash in the waters. She would leave her locket behind on the boat. Rana had held on to the locket for so long as a kind of protection. Now, for Rana, the ashes were not so much about protection. The ashes for Rana were a whole new earth to which she would keep her promises.

ACKNOWLEDGMENTS

I sincerely thank everyone who made this book possible. I dedicate this book to young people everywhere in whom I have great faith. "First, believe in this world – that there is meaning behind everything."

About the author

Shyam R. Gohel (b. April 1, 1982) is working on a new book There's a Flower in your Heart

Cover art by Esther Rai of Sikkim, India

Made in United States
North Haven, CT
25 March 2023